W9-CPC-164

To the memory of Patricia Podriznik,
a warm and wonderful teacher—M.M.S.

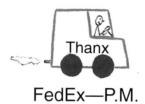

Thanx

FedEx—P.M.

Clarion Books • a Houghton Mifflin Company imprint • 215 Park Avenue South, New York, NY 10003 •
Text copyright © 1997 by Mary McKenna Siddals • Illustrations copyright © 1997 by Petra Mathers •
The illustrations for this book were executed in watercolor on Arches 300-lb. cold-press paper. • The text
was set in 28/34-point Helvetica. • All rights reserved. • For information about permission to reproduce
selections from this book, write to Permissions, Houghton Mifflin Company, 215 Park Avenue South,
New York, NY 10003. • www.houghtonmifflinbooks.com • Printed in Singapore. • **Library of Congress
Cataloging-in-Publication Data** • Siddals, Mary McKenna. • Tell me a season / by Mary McKenna
Siddals ; illustrated by Petra Mathers. • p.   cm. • Summary: Nature displays different colors to
announce the seasons of the year and the time of day. • ISBN 0-395-71021-9 • PA ISBN 0-618-13058-6 •
[1. Seasons—Fiction. 2. Color—Fiction. 3. Bedtime—Fiction.] I. Mathers, Petra, ill. II. Title. • PZ7.S5653Te
1997 • [E]—dc20 • 96-23313 • CIP AC •
TWP 10 9 8 7 6 5 4

Tell Me a Season

by Mary McKenna Siddals
illustrated by Petra Mathers

Clarion Books/New York

brown mud

brown trees

sky of gray

with pink and purple clouds:

Spring morning

yellow sun

blue sky

green
green
green

and rainbow colors:

Summer day

red
yellow

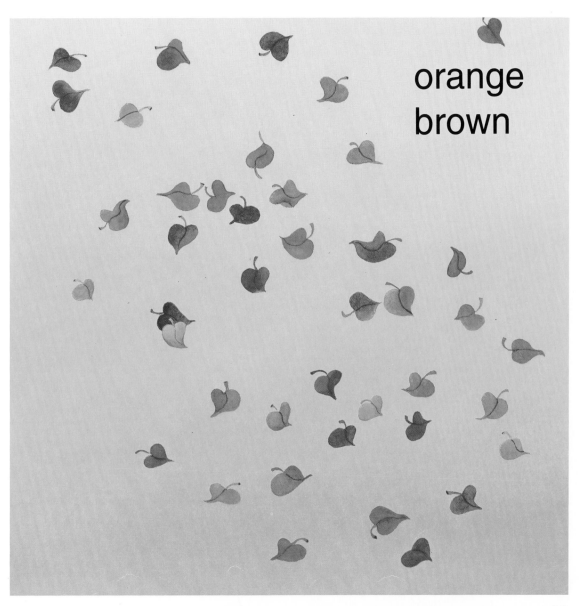

orange
brown

on the trees
on the ground

red and orange and yellow sky:

Fall evening

snow white

shadows black

black sky
white lights

black and white:

23

Winter night

Good night